WHERE ARE YOU GOING, HUMAN?

ZSAZSA K. LOUIS

ARPress

ILLUMINATING IDEAS.
EMPOWERING VOICES

ARPress
45 Dan Road Suite 5
Canton MA 02021

Hotline: 1(888) 821-0229
Fax: 1(508) 545-7580

Ordering Information:
Quantity sales. Special discounts are available on quantity purchases by corporations, associations, and others. For details, contact the publisher at the address above.

Printed in the United States of America.

ISBN-13:   Softcover   979-8-89356-369-6
               eBook   979-8-89356-368-9

Library of Congress Control Number: 2024903088

Life is beautiful, it is a wonder of God
with all its variety, and goodness.

We are all God's children, while we live in a
colorful world with many different kinds

of people. Our life is more complicated than the
surrounding nature, with all its wonders.

People are making life more complicated, and
difficult with lies, hatred, and ugliness.

People are also part of eternity, but they are
not always aware of their importance to
the main.

If they would see it all, they would be better to
one another and have more understanding.

They would not live in sin, with lies,
enviousness, and hatred, because these make life
more difficult, and often unbearable.

Ladislaw's life got shorter by prejudice,
hate, malice, and jealousy, he was left on his own,
and he fought alone against unfavorable odds until he died.

"Each man's death diminishes me,
I am involved in mankind, and therefore,
send not to know for whom the bell tolls, it tolls for thee."

- by John Donne

AUTHOR'S NOTE

L adislaw, the famous gypsy mayor of his village, and one of the most famous Romani activists in Wonderland died under tragic circumstances on 14. July 2020. He was able to change and turn around his whole village in fourteen years with his benevolent, and unorthodox style. He was a man who always lived up to his promises and had a fight against unfavorable odds in his entire life. Even his enemies admitted his positive results, and originality during his negotiations. His lifelong fight against poverty, prejudice, and discrimination was courageous, persistent, and always optimistic. As the leader of his gypsy village, he did his best for the future positive changes, he acted like a good father to his people.

I wrote this book in his best memory for everybody who knew him, and who would like to know him better.

I am from a different "village", and I was happy to come here to the USA and leave behind the sheltered life in the communist system. We decided with my son to move out because we had chosen freedom. I was writing my books on a "pen name" to avoid future harassment for us. I always appreciated the freedom. I fought for justice and equality from my early life, I was always involved with people and their struggles, and I learned from them. My passion is writing, where I can tell my ideas about human relations and look for future positive outcomes. While I started to enjoy the pension, I felt that I owe to give back something to the people who were nice to me, therefore I started to write.

In my old country, I was an attorney for divorce and criminal cases, and I was a tour guide for the neighboring countries in my free time. Here in the USA, I was a card dealer for poker games at 35 years. I also finished my education in the College of South Nevada to be a mental health advisor. I hope I can help more people through my writings. My books are: **"What Happens In Vegas Will Not Stay In Vegas"** contains essays about life in Las Vegas, **"Life-Changing encounters"** about human relationships, and the wrong choices we make, and **"Where Are You Going, Human"** is about Ladislaw, who died under tragic circumstances young and too soon for his endeavor. All the good things he did against discrimination, and for his village as their influential well deserved my work. He was also my hero. This book is to raise awareness of Humanity and avoid suffering from past mistakes and to let people know that "Goodness, love, and understanding" can make miracles.

CHAPTER 1

Ladislaw was a kind and helpful person with a sense of humor therefore people liked him. He got many negative experiences in his life, also tests and trials on his way to his success. He lived on the edge and fought against unfavorable odds in his entire being. His life was the realistic mirror of gypsy's destiny, and the marginalization during their history. Regardless of the odds, he kept his faith for goodness and future positive changes. He was born in a gypsy family in one of the villages of Wonderland in middle Europe, and he lived in a shanty without a bathroom, or electricity with six other people until his eighteen years of age. His parent with four children and grandmother lived in a good understanding together. They did not have high expectations for their life. They just wanted to have enough food to eat, and not to run away, when the police showed up to look for some stolen chicken. They ate from the carcass-well, and occasionally they stole chickens from the neighborhood when their hunger already tortured them. Ladislaw did not have a pair of shoes until he was thirteen years old. He could not go to school, because of their living conditions. He got a slim chance for schooling until his family moved into the city. He got only three years of elementary school. He did not finish his study, because of his family's difficulties. Their whole life was hopeless with many afflictions and disappointments. On a blessed day, his father got hired in the coal-mine, and in a few months, he was the best miner, therefore, a year later, the county provided him with an apartment in the city. Their daily life got better after they had moved, and they also got more support. The mother and the grandmother had high emotional intelligence. They taught their children, much about human relationships. They enlightened their sons about possibilities for their survival, and their chances for the future, when they are going to study, and work. They explained that understanding, and goodness among people help to overcome difficulties and prejudice. Discrimination causes stress, emotional pain, and also mental illness, therefore, they have to behave nice, and understanding. They have to pray that the people will accept them, and they will feel colorblind toward them. In Wonderland, most of the gypsies lived in deep poverty, and they were discriminated at the time being by every other race. They were often the subject of rood jokes and the prejudices of others. Some people had prejudiced them, for stealing, to have less knowledge, or for being less clean. The ruling class did not show any interest to eliminate the differences, through housing, schooling, health care, or other governmental support. Just the opposite. They followed the basic principle for the modern society, of old Roma, "Divide at imperative" means "Divide, and conquer," and they didn't care about the misery of the people. After Ladislaw's family moved to the city in the new apartment, their life got better. The mother showed a good example by cooking tasty food, what she also gave to their neighbors, to please them. They were happy because the children could register for school. Also, the neighbors liked them, because they behaved nicely. In a couple of years, just before they got better with their new life, his father died, and that was a deep emotional shock for the family, especially for the mother, who left alone with the four teenage boys. Ladislaw was the oldest, and when his father died, he took over and went to work for the family because he wanted to avoid starvation. His three younger brothers did the school and helped their mother.

Ladislaw told his mom:

"Please. do not worry I will work hard for our family in the future, that we do not have to snap chicken anymore."

He started in a mechanical appliance factory and worked up in 8 years from yardman to be the director of the produce. He did it step by step with many struggles. He was always nice to everybody, notwithstanding that not everybody was nice to him. The family moved back to their old village after his father's death. They sold their apartment in the city, and they did buy a house for its price. Most of the people in this village were gypsies, and they got a difficult life, with high unemployment, and with high crime rates. Ladislaw helped his people in every way, he had talked to them and did teach them for survival. The village elected Ladislaw to be their mayor. Later a bad turn happened, a new manufacture used Ladislaw's help to rent storage for technical parts in his old village. They paid their price to the village. Ladislaw did not know it, that these parts were stolen. The court gave him for accessory of stealing 2 years, suspended for four years. He did not know that this company operated with stolen goods. Luckily, he did not need to go to jail. He was very sad when he realized that they made him a sucker. Despite the judgment, his village loved him, because of his hard work and straightforward human style. When his people worked on the field, Ladislaw was the first to show them a good example, when they dug out the well, again Ladislaw did it first to save others from an accident to happen. Also, when they produced more, Ladislaw suggested giving away the surplus to the poor, to win their trust and sympathy, especially after their earlier crimes.

They did put signs on the bags:

"We didn't steal it, we produced it to you."

Ladislaw was helping the people of his village in every way. Most of the people were gypsies and had difficulties almost all the time. It was poverty and crime in every corner. Often, they did not have enough money for their living expenses. Ladislaw helped with some money and looked for a job to them. Their homes were old and damaged, and many of them were without water. Ladislaw started to renovate the buildings with his brother Mike and his working team. Mike was a constructor and loved his brother, also their village.

They helped a lot of the people, and they never stopped until they renewed the whole settlement. Ladislaw also used his time to teach the people, especially in winter, when that was frost outside on the fields, and they could not work. They came together on the weekend in the community house, and Ladislaw explained to his people the importance of compliance with the rules, the work expectations, and their adaptation without disturbing anyone, or to show any troublesome behavior. When somebody came late to work or meeting, Ladislaw asked the person to read laud "Winnie the Pooh" and analyze the story. That was the punishment because many of them were shy even to talk and embarrassed.

Ladislaw said:

"I could not fire them because they needed to produce something, at least their living expenses."

Unfortunately, in the beginning, ninety-five percent of the people did not work, and the crime rate was high, most of their activity was stealing. On the list of statistics, they were on the top of their crimes. Ladislaw organized wage labor and community work in public places. His friend, Joe helped him to make many phone calls to workplaces, to find a job for the gypsies. They could not even tell their real names, because if they figured out that the people are gypsies after they told names like Colompar, Ignac, or Orsos, they denied the opportunity from them to work. One day, Ladislaw told the employers about their unfair procedures, and they started to be more helpful. Probably, they were afraid that Ladislaw will talk about them in his next interview, on the TV. He was happy when he could help, and in return, he got love and appreciation. Ladislaw had a big heart, in there took place his whole village, and later the whole country. He instructed the people of the village to live from work, and they did buy the fields around them. They started to produce potatoes and onions.

Ladislaw was a handsome man with goodness, and love in his heart, he was very conscientious, but he never had time to take care of his private life for his good. His family was the people of his village, and they were in the center of his life. To take care of them that was already a big job to fulfill.

He said:

"Goodness, understanding, and love don't cost money, and these help people to overcome difficulties."

The people of the village voted for him to be their mayor, and they did it three times. He served three terms, and he got many medals, among these the Raoul Wallenberg Award in 2020 "For setting an example of humanism, and for his contribution to a peaceful coexistence of minority and majority society." He was one of the best mayors in his country. His district's leaders honored him with a medal also, for that. In May of 2020, he told in his interview that he will never give up his fight for justice. He did fight against poverty, prejudice, and discrimination. Discrimination is

Against the Law in Wonderland, but the people always found a way to ignore the law, and prejudiced against race, and mainly against the unknown. They followed what they heard, not what they experienced.

Ladislaw had always talked to God, and he said:

"I thank you for your trust and goodness my Lord, you gave me a very difficult task, please help me to accomplish your plan for my people, and my whole nation."

He remembered the story of Jonas, who was sent by God to change the people of Ninive. They were all sinners, and God told Jonas to ask them to penitence and to change for the better. Jonas first did not obey God; he was scared to be a prophet. The marines of the cruise-ship did throw him in the sea because they thought he is bad luck. God sent the big whale to swallow Jonas, and he did spend three days in the whale's stomach. He prayed to God for freedom and forgiveness. He promised to fulfill his order. He went to Ninive, but the sinners did not listen to his words, therefore 30 days later Ninive burned down, as God predicted it earlier.

Ladislaw often had felt to be in the stomach of a big whale; alone, helpless, surrounded by walls, and closed out. His steps were difficult from the high responsibility that he carried at the start, and his heart was sad from the prejudice and enviousness of some powerful people. They could not achieve that much result with their public activity, as he did, therefore they were malicious. He was all day long in the service of his people, he did not even have a car to travel to other places to take care of his mission. He was very interested to know about the gypsies living conditions in the whole country because he wanted to help them. He lived alone in his two-bedroom house after he separated from his earlier life partner, Lena. She left because he sacrificed himself for his people and the progress of their village. Ladislaw also got many interviews, because people wanted to know, how could he make the "miracle," to change the whole village in fourteen years, where the gypsies committed earlier many crimes every year, and they did not work regularly in the past. He told the news:

"We did buy the fields and started to produce potato, from what the neighbors lent to me."

"I borrowed it for my watch, and I had to pay it back on time." "Our fields produced so many potatoes, that we could give away the surplus, as a gift to the poor people in the neighborhood."

He continued:

"Believe me the sun rises on the East and setts on the West in our village too, but in between it is very important to treat the people right."

"That is what I did, and I asked them nicely to work for their good."

Some people said, gypsies were known to be lazy, and manipulative, who easily commit crimes, but they don't like to work. Ladislaw proved that is all a prejudice, and he said:

Some people stigmatized the gypsy race by:

"They said, I heard, and I thought."

The people are doing these without knowing who the person is they are talking about, and why her or his life is not in good order. Most of the time bad things are happening because of their miserable living conditions, not because somebody is gypsy.

"There are many hardworking families, in gypsy villages also. The hunger has more cruelty than a sword."

"At the same time goodwill, understanding, and love does not cost money, and these can make "miracles." "When are we going to realize, we are all humans, and we are one nation regardless of our skin colors?"

"I asked my people in the village nicely, like a loving father, and now they are working, because I recognized in them the goodness of any human beings, and I explained to them that study and work are the tools to grow out of human misery. I even visited with them the county jail, to show the consequences of bad behavior." "After successful potato production, we made more than twenty folio-tent to produce prime vegetables for our support, and the giveaway to the poor people. We produced 16 tons in a year." These are the events that changed my people, their changes are in their living conditions.

I learned all these methods from the Internet WEB site, and I shared it with everybody. We also got teachers, not only for agriculture but also for evening classes, that the people could finish elementary school. I went with my people in the school also to finish my education where I left off in my earlier years. In these years, the Census Bureau showed, that four million people are in deep poverty in Wonderland, and three-hundred children died from starvation. Everybody knew that, and its reasons, but the majority of society did not do anything to change that. Only small groups of people were looking for some changes or wanted to help the suffering people. The main reason was that the leading class did not care, because they used the people's money for their pleasure. The president told that his governing style is Christian Democracy because he follows the golden rule, you can expect the same from the people in return, what you provide to them. Also, he made his decisions based on public opinions, and expectations because he wanted to lead democratically. That all did sound good. What about the help from the European Union and what about the people's requests for better housing, more hospitals, and schools? At the same time, they did not do anything for the development of villages, or the poor, and they did even less for the gypsies.

They existed in peripheral, - segregated- hovel colonies, with their autonomy, but their leaders caused more disappointments than development, with few exceptions. They used the people's money for their good and did not help the gypsies to have normal living conditions or to find jobs at all. They did not build schools, or health centers, houses at all. They betrayed their race for more money, and they used it for their interest. Times, when out of ten million people almost half of them are in deep poverty that already shows the government's negative side. They were selfish, corrupt, and impotent. The leaders got a big amount of support from the European Union, but they used the money for corruption, their amusement, and their luxurious life. Some of the hospitals looked like homeless shelters, and they were using the supply several times, while those were for one-time use only. As a result, 30 thousand people died every year, in the related multi-viral infections.

There are no remedies for death, therefore it is reasonable to say that the leaders destroyed many people's life.

The European Union provided the money for the development of impoverished villages, for the renewal of gypsies hovels, for hospitals, and schools. The European Union should lookout, how they did spend their money, and they should require more strict conditions from Wonderland. The government did not care much about poverty, and about the three hundred children, who died from starvation every year. Instead, they acted like those problems are not the government's priorities, or assignments to take care of them. They are all corrupts people's fault and burden. Who was behind the corruption it was never come up? Sadly, also the ruling class was very much involved, and they took their share from the peculated wealth too. Ladislaw detected the problems, and he wanted to change the whole governmental system. He saw that the gypsies-autonomy did not do enough, or anything for the gypsies development, what was required. They were more marginalized with them than before. The gypsy leaders did not have goodwill for their people, instead, they acted like a" Kapo", they made many unjustified arrangements. The European Union's regulations were somewhat casuistic among their members about the financial support not unified yet, therefore a few country leaders of Schengen states played behind the rules. That was the similarity of the gypsy autonomies. They did not respect the requirements, and the rules most of the time.

Ladislaw said:

"We should eliminate the autonomies because the leaders can't be trusted. They are not working for the people's future; they used the support for their interest."

"Also, their hovel's settlements were looking worse than "ghettos", like they are separated to die because the society wanted to close them out."

These were provocative statements, notwithstanding they were very true in most of the situations, but Ladislaw felt that he has to be instrumental for changes.

He said:

"Without understanding and help the gypsies life can't change. We must give a moral bust, also we must treat them as a human, not like an animal. If we want to see development by them, we have to invest in their future, and not stealing their money."

Ladislaw worked day by night for his village, and felt sorry for the people who starved, therefore, they produced tones of vegetables regularly, and they left only as much, as they needed for their survival. They always gave away the surplus to the poor. Some powerful gypsy people were the envy of Ladislaw's success because he was nice, and popular everywhere. He was also on the TV with many interviews. Some gypsy leaders were angry, and hostile, because Ladislaw reviled the truth, and they called Ladislaw a homophobe, racist, and a primitive person. They tried to ignore his results in the development of his village. After they saw the media's possession and frenzy, they started to criticize harshly Ladislaw. They said:

"What this nobody tried to prove, maybe we are not good enough for the gypsies?"

Indeed, that was the case, because they did the same corrupt and impotent leadership to their race, what they experienced by the upper leadership. They were selfish and corrupt. As Ladislaw pointed out, they were always very busy to promise everything, but they did not do anything. They were irresponsible, and liars. The money that they got for the village's development, they used for their interest. They had betrayed their race. They also made sure that the same corrupt, and irresponsible people get elected, and they will rule from time-to-time. That made happy the central power because they could blame the country's misery on the gypsies, as they say:

"Blame on the victim."

One of the European Union's investigation resulted in more than a million dollars deficit in Wonderland. That was the embezzlement of the gypsies money, which they got for the development of their villages from the European Union. There were also places where they rejected the support that they could get to the gypsies development.

They said:

"The gypsies are not responsible enough, therefore they don't count."

At the election time, they gave out a bowl of stew with noodles in return for the gypsy's vote. In this way, nothing happened for a while, only the statistics were devastated. The starving people ate, and they returned to their own hovel's misery, sad and powerless. The leaders were left in their positions to secure the hopeless future for the gypsies. The civil rights protectors could not do too much either, after more than 600 years misery, they legislated the gypsy name does not exist anymore, instead, they are the "minority ethnic group", or Romanis, and gypsy criminology does not exist, as it was earlier, only the criminology as usually. They could not legislate much more for the gypsies, who did not get enough food to eat or have normal living conditions to be able to work or register in the schools. The most important thing to legislate would be " love", but that did not exist toward them for a long time, or maybe never.

Ladislaw thought:

What kind of results are those for the gypsy population after the hardships, insults, and slavery of more than 600 years? They tread them because they did not like them in Wonderland. They were treated like emigrants, and they called them " field Negroes" in their own home because about 58 percent of the population was prejudiced against them. They lived in hovels, without electricity, and water. When they were coming along their way, the white people closed their doors. They did not even want to see them. They felt like they were wasted. They lived from the carcass-well, and some of the casual work; cleaning, basket making, and fortune-telling from hands or cards, if any people wanted to pay for them. What kind of life did they get after many years of discrimination, prejudices, and poverty? What the ruling class did, it was a" hidden genocide" for the gypsy race. They made their life impossible, and shameful because they blamed everything on them. What about the other race, about 3 million people, who were living in deep poverty, who was responsible for that? The dishonest politic of the government was the one. Some of the people in deep poverty got support from the government, but that did not help to change their life. It was enough only to survive their days in hopelessness.

Ladislaw said:

"In a certain period, that was maybe lucrative for the government to revile-abuse-the Jews, the emigrants, the gypsies, the liberals, and so on. Maybe that helped the society to let out the steam, but that was an unjust treatment for those minority groups."

They said gypsies should educate themselves, and work to be accomplished by their own will. Without money, housing, education, healthcare, and information system how can the gypsies exist, or make a step forward, especially in isolated areas? That was nonsense, and everybody knew it. It was a miracle, if someone got on the top as Ladislaw did, thanks also to his good parent. Mostly, the gypsy's upper class made their progress with music when they were lucky to be employed in bigger cities to restaurant's live music, or they got in bands for concerts. They had better chances of living in big cities. The most underdeveloped territories of the country were on the Eastside, and on the South with many poor, mistreated, and depressed people, and they were not only the gypsies. These were the territories, where many people committed suicide every year. The opportunity for gypsies life music was also canceled almost everywhere. The warm human atmosphere with the violin and gypsies bands were gone with the wind. The gypsy musicians only could work by private's invitation for some weddings, or funerals. In earlier years, it was the main attraction for tourists to go to gourmet restaurants with gypsy's music, because they got a free concert during their tasty dinner, for the same price. These days were over, and the gypsies, who got higher education, could change to be security guards, janitors, or cleaning technicians in big companies if they were lucky. It was hard to survive these kinds of regulations for people who were talented musicians, but in Wonderland the leaders ignored, how the people did feel after these kinds of changes. Only the leader's reactions were somewhat important when the president let build stadiums, ridings halls, and yachts at the Adrian seaside, everybody played "blind and deaf." The "non-existing" football heroes could not appreciate the stadiums. The four millions of impoverished people did not have money to enjoy the riding-halls. Everybody was amazed by their irresponsible acts, but they did not do anything to repair their arrangements.

The government even did borrow money from the pension fund, which is against the regulation. The question remains, when are they going to pay it back? The people were scared about their future and said:

"It seems that the elderly, the poor, and the gypsies don't count in our country."

Some of the people made jokes, about the stadiums like:

"Next time, when I am sick, I will go to the stadium to find a doctor for my cure."

Other people said the president made our country his "Hobby-land" with attractions which only he and his close friends could enjoy. They got the big money,

and how, that could be a sad story.

Some people who were more philosophers, or smarter said:

"Our President didn't tell yet only one thing that" Poverty in Wonderland is Prohibited."

Maybe, that could be his best ruling so far because he started it with the homeless population. He said: "It is forbidden to be in public places for the homeless." It means, gets out of the streets with the homeless people, maybe they should learn how to fly. While some politicians talked about stabilizing the civil democracy, they left out their share, and their contribution to the important expenses, notwithstanding that some of their friends developed to be millionaires with their connections to the leaders, in a very short time. The new millionaires could do many things for the community, but they were selfish, money-hungry, and corrupt. Shortly, they were not that kind at all.

Maybe the leaders didn't learn the old saying yet:

"It is nice to be important, but more important to be nice."

The banks and financial institutions got in bankruptcy and left without money, therefore the trust broke, and again the people got disappointed by their irresponsible procedures. Without paying back the costumer's life earnings, it was a very bad surprise for many people, but they could not do anything about it. The money, that some leaders embezzled was for schools, hospitals, also for the development of the gypsies hovels to regular apartments, in the villages. One of the leading gypsy representatives disappeared after the European Union investigations, who should organize the development of the gypsies hovels. Instead, he embezzled the money, with some others, who also disappeared, or got secretly killed. After these events did nothing happen. People said:

"They knew who did the embezzlement, and for how much. It was proven, and they didn't do anything to get back the money for the gypsies developments, while they were suffering from hunger."

That did hurt the whole population with its consequences. After that, the leaders "Washed their hands. "They could not preserve the trust after these situations by the population, and the gypsies were very sad about their "non-existing" future.

Ladislaw detected the pain and suffering of his people. He helped in every way he could. In one of his interviews, he told them, they had built a new community house in their village, and the people can come together every week to talk about their experiences and problems. He educated his people about many important things in society, also about their work, and adaptive behavior. He explained the importance of skills development and informed them about society's measures. Ladislaw told when they do anything for their progress, they must find a solution by not to bother or irritate other people around them, to be able to avoid arguments. Also, he told them to be proud of the results of their productivity and goodness, while they gave away the surplus of their products to the poor every year.

Ladislaw said:

"Only the people who have can give away some products."

"We always have to help the people who are less fortunate, and needy."

"I am very proud of all of you because you did your best. Thank you much for that."

Ladislaw together with the people of his village wanted also build trust with their neighbors, therefore, they made a symbol, a" friendship- bridge," that the people can come over from the neighborhood to visit, exchange ideas, and learn from their good example. They did not only renovate their houses, but they had built playgrounds for the children, and they planted trees, and flowers. They regularly gave away tones of produce for the poor people by near and far. Their crime rate also dropped down from yearly six hundred only to 5-6 crimes in a year. The whole country heard about this village, and they got surprised about the many good things, they did.

Ladislaw told:

"We have to employ the demand in people's lives for their future and teach them to appreciate others. I also want everybody to feel at home in our village."

Ladislaw was honored with the humanity prize, but some people of the upper gypsy organizations were angry with him, because he did not follow their footsteps, and he did not trust much about their help or in the changes of certain rules. Instead, he faced with the daily reality, and he made big changes with his people on their own in their village. In his next interview, Ladislaw told that his race condemned him to be nice, and they spit on him, also kick him from the back when he walked out of a meeting in the capital. They also tried to hit him with the car by his road crossing, to kill him. That was ugly, and very far from fairness, and then Ladislaw concluded:

"I am not angry, because I think they are envy. They can't see the reality."

Enviousness is living with us for longer than two thousand years. We need to have criticism for ourselves first. We must live without revenge and malice.

"The eye for an eye principle made blind people, that is not the right way." -he told.

It seemed that he needed to fight also with some leaders of his race, who were ignorant for many things, also corrupt, and unjust.

"In the Bible, Kain killed his brother Abel for enviousness", -said Ladislaw.

"That is a bad motivation, love, and understanding of other human beings are much better."

Everybody was shocked when Ladislaw got two more international prizes for his work and humanity. Also, the UNO-United Nation's Organization- invited him to talk about the gypsies race problem. The German government and Vienna also invited him to talk about the gypsies, and about his village's development. After all the hostility, and humiliating reactions seemed to be scary to stay in office, as a representative of the gypsies, and the poor, but Ladislaw was not scared.

He told:

"I am very sad that some people are intolerant, liars, and cruel, they don't understand goodness, as they should. Some of them are also influenced by their fear." "The gypsies will not disappear from one day to the next. It would not be better when they can fit in the society, and not closed out?"

I will not disappear in the "Bermuda Triangle" to ease some people's minds and worries."

"It would be better to work together on the differences, that could help for our future because gypsies are not a problem but assignment, which we have to settle together."

"I never saw any gypsy to wake up in the morning, and would decide to do something bad, they all wanted to be good, and they all wanted to live in happiness." "Happiness is the natural choice of any human being, but nobody can choose which family will be born. We are not able to change our race and origin."

"God wanted us this way, to be diverse but to be kind to one another. as the bible said:

"Love one another, and do to others, as you want them to do to you, first of all, love God."

-explained Ladislaw in one of his interviews.

He was right, and he was already hurting from his fights, and from the many negative experiences he got. One of the TV stations invited him to have a twin interview with the priest.

In the beginning, the priest cited the pope:

"The cry of the poor is getting stronger every day, yet every day it is less heard."

The reporter asked Ladislaw, how was he able to convince the people, especially the gypsies to work in their village, or some of them, who had revolted against his ideas, and orders.

Ladislaw said:

"They called me out to a boxing match, I didn't have a choice, I did fight."

The priest asked him:

"Did you remember to the old Christian saying: "Better to give, than take.""

Ladislaw said:

"I did, but their particular problem was my role."

"They probably wanted to see, if I am strong enough to lead, and to cope with daily reality."

"These kinds of problems are all gone. Now, we work together for our future."- add Ladislaw

Everybody was wondering that he was correct in all his answers, and talked soft, and nice.

In one of his interviews he told that on the way home, he is often crying inside because he is hurting from the cruelty of some people.

Ladislaw said:

"In Wonderland's history, there were many bad things, and some people didn't learn from the past at all. Despite prejudices, the gypsies were always voluntarily at the side of their country in many fights- in war, or revolution- in the past."

Also, they have the holiday for the Holocaust on the Second of August, to remind the people what Hitler did to the gypsies, besides many other people. They deported and killed many thousands of them. This day is a symbol of remembering racism in more than twenty countries in Europe. It would be time to repair the many bad things, that they did against humanity. Ladislaw told in one of his interviews that he wants to organize a quiet demonstration, as a reminder of humanity in August for all the gypsies in the country, with the sign:

"We are also human beings, we are one nation".

Some of his friends warned him, maybe that could bother the ruling class. They will find it dangerous when all the unhappy people, will add to the crowd. That may lead to a revolution against the ruling class for the many unfair arrangement and corruption, what the people already knew.

"God has been always at my side, and I hope I will be able to do it."-answered Ladislaw for these warnings and then he said:

"I have to wake up the people for today's reality, fear is not an option for me."

At earlier years, and months there were several bloody fights among the gypsies, and between the gypsies and the white people with very sad results in different territories of the land. The leaders washed their hands, as always without doing anything. Many people died for no good reason on each side, and the ruling class did not say much about it. Like it is not unusual. Wonderland's government overlooked its responsibility again, and blamed everything on the gypsies, except in one case where some white people used bombs, and machine guns to kill innocent gypsy families, with their children, who run out of their houses. These families were working, and their children went to the school regularly, but some heartless people did not care, because of their hate, and prejudice. They got their sentences for life terms because for the European Union's members the death sentence did not exist. The whole country found tragic and strange the situation. Everybody was wondering, where these individuals could get bombs, and machine guns. Officially those belonged to the military, it was the question, who provided those for the terrorist. After all of the misery of race discrimination, and four million starving people, that is what Wonderland's president said:

"In the last hundred years, the last ten was the best, because we made steps forward. We created from the " welfare" society supplied by the European Union, a" workfare" society for our country. Their money for support was not beneficial, because they tried to undermine our politic and independence. We gave back the earlier borrowed money to the European Union for our future. They gave us the money, like:

"Here is a hump for the lame."

I did fight for our country's interest that the emigrants can't come in if we do not want them. I do not have anything against them, but we are a small country, and we have enough problems on our own without them. The European Union tried to influence our country's economy for their interest, and they wanted us also to take in emigrants. We fought with my cabinet, that some western millionaires can't buy our " Owings" from the banks, and financial institutions. Through these actions, they can't own our country. The president never said anything about the more than millions of dollars, what one of their main politicians embezzled from the gypsy's development. He did not explain anything about the four million impoverished people's future, out of the ten million, who lived in Wonderland. The three-hundred children per year, who starved to death were not mentioned in his speech either. About the infectious diseases in hospitals, and about the deteriorating conditions he also forgot to tell, while 30 thousand people died in a year in infectious diseases. He told the people that the unemployment rate changed because they got 860 thousand new job opportunities. If that was true or made up, nobody would know it. Many people also blamed him to change important rules of society for their interests. Also, many homeless people ended up in court and jail, while many of them got on the street with the leader's heartless arrangements. Most of their rules, and regulations what the president changed, were in the favor of the ruling class, and not in favor of the average citizens. He told that he was proud of the many Nobel prize winners, and the many gold medals winners of the Olympics in Wonderland, but those prizes had nothing to do with him or his activity. It had sounded as he did it. Some people would think he wanted to make the impression on the nation, instead of his "achievements", what he failed to do. After considering these facts, his speech was amusing, but not realistic, or true at all. Maybe some people with fewer experiences believed it, but many people were in doubt, and scared, what else can happen in the future.

During history, Wonderland was famous for many things, but for sure not about its leaders. They were irresponsible with their governing style, and with their citizen's money, whereas most of them had great rhetorical skills, also bravery but they were without positive results. Either they team up with the wrong partners, or they were too easy-going with their population's assets and future. By the way, also the election's circumstances were somewhat shady and unfair for the leader's platform. Many people did not know about it. They invited earlier citizens from foreign countries to vote for them. Also, people who already died voted in letters. From one address they received 2000 votes. That was a private place, not a factory or institution. Regardless they did not live in Wonderland, because they were fictitious, they voted for the people who lived there, to enjoy the results of their election. Some of them, who did live outside of Wonderland voted for " favors" of any kind.

CHAPTER 2

It was a hot autumn afternoon in the small village, and some gypsy children were playing together in the shade of the big oak tree, a couple of feet from the brook. They usually took a bath, in the brook when the weather was warm. The children collected stones to throw in the water. The girls had some old Christmas ornaments on the thread, and they asked:

"Where did I hide it, maybe you can find it?"

Ladislaw had a serious conversation with the boys, about what kind of future they can have, while they tried to throw the stones in the water very far.

Lena's brother Anton told:

"I stick with my violin, and I hope they will employ me in a gypsy band soon."

"I will be a civil rights activist, and I will fight for my gypsy race, that they will not starve anymore."-said Ladislaw.

One of his friends, Nick said:

"I think you will sooner marry Lena and have children than go and fight for anybody."

Ladislaw said:

"We are going to see it."

Suddenly the police arrived, and the policeman asked them:

"Why are you not in school?"

Ladislaw was the oldest, thirteen years old, and he politely answered:

"We don't have shoes to walk that far, but hopefully next week our parent can buy shoes, and we will go."

The policeman said:

"I do not want to see you here when there is school time."

In Wonderland, the children were obligated to go to the school until 16 years of age, otherwise, they fined the parent. The gypsies "income" was less, it did not even reach the minimum wage, because they could not find a job, only occasionally. To penalize them could be heartless. Ladislaw told his mom, what did happen. His mom was a nice person who never used bad words or said bad things about anybody.

She said:

"God bless the police, they are doing their job. They also have responsibility for the children. If you do not visit the school at least until you be 16 years old, they fine the parent, but we are lucky. They did not do that. Our poverty can't be an excuse. We will buy a pair of shoes soon, and you will go with your brothers to school. It is very important to learn about your future."

They were lived on casual work when they could find one. The youngsters went to steal chicken at night when hunger knocked on their door. That was dangerous and very humiliating, but they could not starve, as long time, as their budget got finally better. They also had problems with the dressing codes and some of their undisciplined behavior. Not many people recognized that they need help in every way, instead of judging them. Nicely put, without help, they were not always suitable to attend the school. Ladislaw got his lucky day when his daddy was employed in the coal mine, and a year later his district provided for him and his family a new build apartment in the city for his good work. From that day on, Ladislaw could register with his brothers in the school. They were all very happy, especially Ladislaw, because he also got a pair of shoes. It was a very big question if the schoolmates will accept them in the lower class because they should attend with their age already in the higher class. Lena was the best looking among the girls, and she wrote on the blackboard:

"I am not gypsy, only my mom, my dad, and the others are."

The white children cracked out, and they liked Lena, but not the others. They were seated in the last line like they are not good enough for the class. That was the teacher's prejudice because they did not want to hurt the feelings of the white race. That should not happen for the children's sake, because of the peaceful coexistence. They got many hard times, and difficulties, but at least they all could learn the basics: read and write, also mathematics. Ladislaw's father worked at the night shift; therefore, he could meet only on his day-offs with his sons. Every Sunday, their mother took them to the church, and they had seats in the last line not to bother anybody. They went to the church to get forgiveness for their sins and listen to the nice songs. One of the brothers Jon had a nice voice, and he liked to sing. Ladislaw prayed for help to God also, because the school seemed to be very difficult, but Lena helped him because she learned already to write. Their mother and grandmother tried to motivate the boys to study for their future. They promised donuts with marmalade for the weekend if their grades will be good. Their mother was a great cook, she always gave away food to the neighbors to show benevolence, good example, and build up their trust. She cooked chicken soup when somebody got sick in the neighborhood, and she gave it to their family. Luckily, they liked Ladislaw's family, and they did not look at them, like gypsies. One of the happiest days for Ladislaw was when Lena's brother invited him to his concert in the city's Music-hall. The only problem was, how can he get to the Music-Hall. One of his neighbors liked them to be helpful, and he took them to the Music-Hall with his car. They were all proud, and happy. The concert was beautiful, and they played virtuoso the Liszt's Rhapsody, that was for Ladislaw like to be in Heaven. On Saturdays, daddy took the boys to fish to the upper channel of the brook, close to the mountain, where the water was deeper. Occasionally, some smaller fishes swam by. They got a big basket, with donuts, apple, and drinking water for the whole day. They also got the fishing net to catch the fish. There was a forest on the way to the brook, and they looked for the linden-tree to collect its flowers for winter to make lime blossom tea. This tea was very useful against cold and coughing also helped with the heart's beat for elderly people. On the way to the mountain, they collected mushrooms, blueberry, plum, and rosehip. Grandma liked to cook marmalade, and the rosehip was used also for tea. The road was long, and sweaty because of the long walk, but it was very lucrative for the family, with the fruits they found. On the way back, they also found a walnut tree, with many nuts. They saw deer, rabbits, and a lot of birds. They could find everything, but not any fish.

Daddy said:

"Even, when I am tired, I am happy to be in the forest, for me nature is a cure against stress. With its wonders, it makes me feel always free, and happy."

"How you like it guys?"

Ladislaw said:

"It is good that nature provided for us many things, and I also like to listen to the birds."

"What can we take home for dinner, that is still a problem. We can't return empty-handed."

Daddy said:

"We have to look for gopher, mom can cook stew out of them. Rabbits are too fast to catch."

They found a few, but Ladislaw was sad about them. Also, Mike started to cry for the little sweet creatures. When daddy did not look at them, they let go of free the gophers. They had put a frog in the basket instead. When they got home it was evening already. Their mom did look into the basket, but only a big frog jumped out from the fruits and green stuff, what they got on the bottom. The mushroom was good for cooking, so mom made scrambled eggs with onion and mushroom. She also fried some potatoes. That was a good dinner without the gophers also.

Daddy said:

"These boys could be good, as a baby-sitter somewhere, because they worried more about the gophers than about our dinner. They let them go free."

The next Saturday was sad for the family, it was no excursion in the forest. Suddenly, Ladislaw's father died. That was bewildering for all of them, especially for the mother with the teenage boys. They were crying, and they were very sad for a long time. After their father's death, they sold their apartment and moved back to the old village where they had to buy a family home. Not to have the earlier misery without the money, Ladislaw was looking for a job right away. He was young, nice, and very polite. He was eighteen years old, and everybody loved him. They hired him in the technical appliance factory, as a porter, a yardman to clean. He needed to walk 20 kilometers to the city that day because they were out of the money again, and he could not ride with the bus. Ladislaw worked diligently, and one day the boss asked him:

"Why did you not clean up all the cigarette-stub from the back-yard?"

Ladislaw politely answered:

"The people always throw out more after I cleaned it, and for my eight hours shift, I didn't have enough time for that many butts to clean again."

Then for the boss's surprise, he showed mathematically the details in numbers to the seconds and the daily consumption of cigarettes.

He was right, and then he said:

"I am sorry, but I have only my two hands for my eight hours, it seems that is my handicap."

Ladislaw's boss was smiling, and he told him, that the next day he will work in the packaging section because he is very good at mathematics. Ladislaw was happy, and he had run to Lena to tell the good news.

He said to her:

"Lena, I will be okay with my job, therefore my baby, we will live together next month, or I will marry you if we have enough money for that."

Lena said:

"For love, we don't need papers, we better save our money for hard times."

"We will ask our priest for the blessing of our engagement on Sunday."

Ladislaw said:

"I love you, and I always will."

Lena said:

"I love you, even more, you are my man forever."

Ladislaw did tell his mom about his engagement's plan with Lena, and the mother said:

"I love Lena, she is a nice girl, but I think you should finish school first because you did only three classes."

Ladislaw said:

"For me, life is the best teacher, because I don't feel comfortable with my age among young children in the class. I had grown out of it. I can do it later."

Mom said:

"If that is how you feel, go ahead with Lena."

Mom invited Lena with her family on the weekend for engagement dinner. She cooked half of the day, and the food was delicious. She also made strudel with cabbage. She put up candle lights on the table in their garden, and she got a bottle of wine from the neighbors.

Lena and Ladislaw had sitting in the middle of the table, and mom prayed, as daddy used to do it before dinner:

"Please our Lord: Bless the food before us, the family beside us, and the love between us. Give us peace, love, and happiness always, Amen."

Lena and Ladislaw kissed one another and sent a kiss to everybody. They were all happy, and smiley, and they enjoyed the tasty food. The young couple wanted to live with mom until they save money for an apartment. As time went by, Lena always was at Ladislaw's side in good, and bad situations. He was looking for other money-making possibilities, but in the factory now they made him a leader, a director of produce. Ladislaw prayed to God to give him strength, and a good understanding of the people's problems. Everybody could turn to him with any kind of problem, at any time. He also fired some people either for their lies, sloppiness, or sloppy performances. That made him sad because he gave a fair warning to these people before that happened. One day a new company provided parts for appliances, and they were very good with their delivery. They always arrived on time. During these days Ladislaw got elected to be the mayor of his village. He was happy when this new company asked him to provide storage for their parts in the village. Ladislaw thought: the money they will pay, can be used for his village's development. When all was completed and paid, he learned that those people were criminals. They used Ladislaw's nativity and unexperienced manner for their benefit. Ladislaw missed to looking after them before the deal. Ladislaw got 2 years jail term, suspended for four years, for accessory to stealing. He was very sad, and he didn't know how to tell his people in the village. They forgave him because they knew him, and they felt his love in everything he did for them. It bothered him that they made him a sucker for this storage.

Lena said:

"Regardless of what they say, I know that you are a good man, and you were thinking about the future of the village. That is not your fault that they were criminals." "I am sure you will watch more carefully the next time before any cooperation."

To ease up from his pain, Ladislaw decided to go to the neighboring village's fair. He wanted to buy a big umbrella for the garden, to have shade behind the house there. Lena was very happy because she also wanted to have earrings and a bracelet from beads. At the fair, they got many clothes, cheap furniture, fruits, old pictures, and old accessories also were there. Lena could find nice blue earrings very cheap, and Ladislaw got the umbrella. It was a little bit faded but still in working condition. They made good bargains. They ate ice cream and left home happy. Ladislaw's mom was also happy because she liked to seat in the garden in the afternoons, but she missed the shade. Ladislaw did also buy a ball to play with his brothers. On Monday, the following morning Ladislaw woke up early, and he planned for their village's production. He was very excited about it. While he started to work on the development of their village, and he saw that his people are somewhat helpless, and needy, he was considering buying fields. They did buy the fields a few weeks later for agriculture. The village started first to produce a lot of potatoes, and onions. From the surplus, they gave back first what they borrowed, and the rest they gave away to the poor people of the neighboring villages. They kept only as much, as they needed to live on it. After his big lesson and disappointment over the criminal's company's rent, Ladislaw tried to do, even more. They made the folia tents for prime vegetables, and they planted more trees, and flowers in their village to build up the resident's self-confidence, and for their daily pleasant environment. One of Ladislaw's brother, Mike was a constructor, and he helped Ladislaw to organize people for the reconstruction of their houses to renew their village and win the neighbor's sympathy, and trust. They also renovated their church beautifully. After they renovated the old buildings, the look of their whole village changed. People started to visit their village. They wanted to know, how the gypsies made these many changes. Behind all the positive changes there was a man, who sacrificed his whole life for his people. That was Ladislaw. He was an initiator and a leader in the positive meaning of it. He always informed his people about every important step and event around them, and he had helped them. In wintertime, they could not work on the fields, and therefore Ladislaw educated his people daily in their community house about the facts of life for several hours. When they celebrated Christmas, Ladislaw made sure that every child got a gift, even just a simple one, because they could not afford an expensive one. Ladislaw wrote a nice poem to the village about understanding among people. Prejudice by the white race in the neighboring villages happened every day because they had also remembered the time, when the gypsies had stolen, and they did not work.

Ladislaw said:

"Human relationships are like our plantations for future good, we must cultivate them."

The poem what Ladislaw wrote, was very touchy, and had four chapters, like these:

We are torn by the wind in the same way,
We are hit by the rain in the same way,
We are burned by the sun in the same way,
We are numbed by the frost in the same way.
We are called by our father in the same way.
We are loved by our mother in the same way,
why can we not understand one another in the same way?"
Yes, that was the sad truth,
because the prejudice existed by many people of the land.
When will they going to repair the many mistakes they made,
and when they will give help to avoid the starvation and the
loveless society?
When will the ruling class recognize finally, that hate causing
more problems also for them, therefore, they should calm down
the people,
and not instigate racist ideas, or fights among the people.
They should consider the future more seriously in the interest of
the whole nation.

Many reporters said:

"The people needed more Ladislaw's kind of schemes, and his loving management for the left-out people, and for people from other races to make changes."

Ladislaw said:

"They need most of all goodwill to help for the less fortunate people in the country."

"Believe me, there are many Ladislaws, and they are just waiting for their chances to lead."

After several interviews and medals, he got an insulting letter from the leader's son, as follow:

"What do you think about yourself, you" little nobody"? You will ever belong to the political "elite". I will show it to you."

Ladislaw answered:

I am sorry that you show a bad example for the people, as the leader's son. I am not going to insult you, as you did. I can promise you only one thing, that I will always fight against poverty, and prejudice of the people until I live, and I can move. I do not want to belong to the "elite" class or any party, I am satisfied when I can help my people. I think you should learn more respect. I wish you, and your family happiness, always"-Ladislaw.

His letter was amazing, after the arrogancy what the leader's son showed toward Ladislaw.

Interestingly, a few months later the leader's son, showed up with his friends in the streets of the capital, as a preacher, and as a messenger of Jesus. They wanted to convince the people about his goodness, and thoughtfulness toward the poor. He acted like an impostor, he fooled the people around him about his benevolence, while he wrote his ugly letter to Ladislaw, just because he had good results in his village, and he was the envy of Ladislaw's success. That was preposterous by all its meaning and measures. This is the beginning of the end of humanity, and the apocalypse, if he is the representative of Jesus. He never represented goodness. He and his whole family were arrogant and corrupt. -said the person on the sidewalk, while he was listening to his speech. The people who did not know much about him, and their politic, or did not have Internet, they believed what he said. After all the hostility, and humiliating reactions seemed to be scary to stay in office, as a representative of the gypsies, and the poor, but Ladislaw was not scared.

He said:

"Thank God, I am living in a beautiful, and free country, and people who are in disbelieve, and uninformed do not bother me, my job is to convince everybody," Ladislaw explained:

"I am not scared, I think someone has to wake up people to act, fear is not an option for me."

Ladislaw got his invitation to the United Nation's Organization also, to talk about the gypsy's race's main problems. He was in a high stress, and prayed to God, he said:

"Our Lord, I know my weakness to be often impatient, please forgive me, and help me to be true to my people and help them for the good changes. Thank you, Lord." He was talking about the missing self-criticism, and about their discrimination of women, and also other races. He said:

"Every new step starts with self-criticism, and we are not exceptions either." "All the leaders should help to solve the gypsy's race impoverished situation."

At home, the gypsy leaders got angry, because he communicated openly about his observations, as a leader of his village. Some other gypsy leaders did not sympathize with his ideas to eliminate the gypsies autonomies at all. At the next meeting, he got called on names, like a homophobic, primitive, traitor of their past, and so on. That was very sad, but happened, because he was against the self-autonomy, whereas that was a "blind leading blind" organization for the gypsies. He made up his mind by the gypsy leader's irresponsible, corrupt, and impotent leadership. They were money-hungry and unprofessional. They were not right, or fair. Any change in human beings must start with self-criticism. That these leaders did not have.

Ladislaw went on his way, and his village elected him also two more times to be their mayor. At this time, he got another medal for his humanity, but this did not make a difference the way he lived his life. He had more interest in his village than in medals.

He made round calls every morning to ask the elderly people if they need help with anything. He talked to his people about their daily work also in every morning, because he wanted to make sure that everybody knows their daily assignment. He started to work with a graffiti artist, on the back wall of his office, and he made a memorial for the victims of the Holocaust there. He also invited a judo instructor to train the teenagers to learn the sport and learn the fight for their protection. He paid the instructor's salary from his pocket.

Things were going less great with his private life because he did not get enough time for his-self. He lived with Lena at twenty-seven years, but they did not get children, and Ladislaw wanted children. They broke up their relationship, but the love always stayed between them, and they were still friends. Ladislaw was very busy, and he was called almost every other week for an interview, everybody was interested very much in his methods, and his work to success. The people of the whole country knew about him, and respected him, while he unselfishly shared his secrets to success with anybody, and everybody, who needed it. The reporters visited the village and they were surprised by seeing the village's production, and the many good things they accomplished. Ladislaw thought their example will be a good model for the other gypsies, and the poor villages, when they will see it on the TV program, or hear about it. Ladislaw always invited the reporters to gypsy's dinner, made by his mother to make a lasting impression for the village's future. His friends liked Ladislaw because he was happy, and he liked to joke with them. They came together to play football-soccer-on the field. They brought beer for the occasion. Ladislaw closed the hunky-tank, because he wanted his people to focus on their daily work, and not on the alcohol. Nobody opposed it, they could buy drinks and enjoy it at home with their family.

He got a new love; her name was Mimi. She was beautiful and carrying, she loved Ladislaw, and she wanted to be his partner in all his plans. She helped Ladislaw in organizations of meetings, and other programs, she wanted to know always about Ladislaw's day, and about his plans. They were organizing the people's work on the weekends for a seasonal job in other people's fields, that they can have extra money for their living, to buy animals, cars, to go to the evening schools, and so on. All the children from their village studied very diligently because Ladislaw always showed interest in their grades and well-being.

He used to say:

"Are you going to study hard to be my doctor, when I am old and sick?"

One of the children Lilla answered:

"We love you, therefore you are never going to be sick."

One day he took the boys with the parent to visit the county jail. He wanted them to experience the humiliation at first hand.

He said:

"I want you to learn from it, and lead your life accordingly, without these kinds of negative experiences."

"You have to remember always that you are the architect of your future."

The next time, he went with the girls to see the university to have the right idea about their future.

Ladislaw said:

"Please, do not hurry to twist your life with early childbirth, you must develop your ability, and your knowledge first to be a responsible mother, and raise good children, who will be never starving."

No wonder, that the people of his village loved Ladislaw because he acted like a responsible father in their best interest, all the time. Sadly, there were people in the Better party, who hated him for his popularity and his fight for the gypsies. One day, they pursued him on the street on his way home.

They were the skinheads and they said:

"What's up gypsy King, are you alone?"

Ladislaw said:

"You can beat me up but first hear me out."

"I didn't have a choice where I want to be born, and I am a gypsy. Believe me, I was chosen to be the mayor because they trusted me."

"The only thing I can do now to fight for my people and help them to live."

"We are all different, maybe you hate me, but I don't hate you."

After what he said the skinheads got surprised, and in shame, therefore they let him go. Mimi waited for Ladislaw in his office because she wanted to go with him to the secondhand shop to buy shirts, and shoes and whatever looks new. Ladislaw had less time and money for these things. Mimi also liked the way Ladislaw was joking about some pieces, when she tried on, like these:" You look like Minci pooh, with this big sweater, you look like a salon girl, in the red blouse, with a deep cut, and so on." That was an amusing show for Mimi. Ladislaw did not say anything about the skinheads, he wanted to avoid Mimi's sadness. They were happy together, and they went for dinner at Ladislaw's mom's house later. She cooked very tasty gypsy food and made an inviting table for them. Mimi was blond and very shy, but she got a beautiful face.

Ladislaw told her:

"You are my Guardian Angel, my happiness, and everything. I hope our life will be nice together, with many children. So far, I could have only my brother's children at Christmas around me. Next Christmas I would like to see our child with us."

Mimi was smiling, and she answered:

"Trust me, I am going to be on it."

Both laugh after these and kissed. Later, they talked about building a new processing center for canned goods, because of the vegetable's surplus, that they produced.

Ladislaw said:

"I only have the money for the two-third of the processing center. Hopefully, I will be able to borrow the rest from the bank. The products will have the name "Lasipe", it means goodness. That will be a reminder for the people to love one another, and not judge."

The only uncertainty I have about our demonstration in August, because of the central power. They might want to hinder it because they are afraid that the people will revolt against poverty, and their ignorant, and humiliating governing style.

Ladislaw continued his speech:

"I believe that the people have to know the truth, that the government wheedled them out of their money, and through their starvation, also out of their life." "They exploited their situations for money at any time they could do it."

"Many people don't know that one point two million gypsies in Wonderland live in medieval conditions, in a very vulnerable situation, and they are desperate for their life. Many of them even denied their race, to have less pain.

No wonder the statistics are not correct. The people, in more than 300 settlements live in hovels, and they do not have water, electricity, or a normal life condition in the twentieth century. These people are not all gypsies, more than half of them are white people. They are losing their power of faith, because they are unemployed, and they do not have any help or any hope for anything." The rules for better living conditions by the European Union are not effectuated in the poor people's daily life and even less for the gypsies. That was also the autonomy's leader's responsibility, and fault, because they are the puppets of the government.

As some said:

"The gypsies don't count."

Mimi told; as I heard:

"That is also the fault of the government, because some powerful people embezzled from them the provision what was for their development, and they left them without future help."

"The same time some people when they did not like the government's doing, they are already disappeared."

Ladislaw's mother said:

"Better we keep our mouth shut because it can be dangerous to talk."

Ladislaw said.

"We always got to tell the truth, mama, regardless of consequences."

"We lived too long in fearful societies; it is time for us to tell the truth."

"The rules alone can't change society, we have to do it based on the needs of the people."

They said thank you for the dinner, gave a big hug to mama, and walked home, hand in hand.

Mimi said to Ladislaw:

"You know that I am in love with you, please, do not say, or do any foolish."

Ladislaw said:

"Promise me one thing in case I die you will go forward on my way. You will find helpers, and you will complete, where I left it off without fear."

"Don't forget, the gypsies need somebody to be able to help them to grow out of their more than 600 years of misery."

Mimi started to cry, and she said:

"I wish, the world would know what a great heart you got, and what a nice human being you are."

"I love you very much, and I always will."

Ladislaw said:

"I pray for my people, in my country to wake up one day free. They will be free from their fear, and their prejudices."

The next day, the priest came over to see the Holocaust picture, and he was pleasantly surprised by the talent of Ladislaw. He had promised to Ladislaw when his work is completed, he shall return for the blessing of their nice, artistic memorial.

The priest said to Ladislaw:

"Hate is our greatest enemy that kills our soul and turns us against one another."

"Do not forget, wisdom is also living in our soul."

"I saw in the Census Bureau's statistic about the 300 settlement, where the people live in deep poverty, and I also visited a few. That was very depressing and sad."-told the priest.

Ladislaw answered:

"We can't give up before we succeed, I gave my life for my people."

The priest gave a ride to Ladislaw in the capital because he went to a civil rights protection meeting with some higher gypsy leaders.

The priest said:

"I am sure that they are the envy of you because they can't show as much result about the past ten years like you did."

Ladislaw said:

"Enviousness is living with us for more than two-thousands years. I am not expecting anything. Probably, they will try to prove that I am nobody compares to them."

The priest said:

"You read my mind, I thought the same, I just didn't want to make you worry."

"God be with you always, my son."

"Thank you, much"-said Ladislaw, and gave a friendly hug to the priest before he left.

This meeting was a big disappointment for Ladislaw because some of the people said worse and unjust things about him. Also because of the short time, he did not get a chance to answer his opponent's unjust accusations.

One of the speakers said:

"You are irresponsible, because you talked about all the gypsies, while you lead only four hundred of them in your village. Why do you think, you have the right to say anything about the number of gypsy criminals when you visited only three jails? Why do you search the garbage of your people in the village to proving, what kind of living cost they have? This is humiliating on the top of other problems".

Ladislaw answered:

"After many complaints of childcare, I wanted to show them, that they spend their money on tobacco, and alcohol more than on the child. I wanted to protect the children's support before I give them more community support. I do not want to humiliate anybody just know the truth for fairness."

This representative of civil rights also asked:

"How comes that you are liked so much by the reporters on the TV?"

"I will tell you, because you prove, what they want to hear."

Ladislaw said:

"You should ask them first, and I was not coming here, or go anywhere to prove anything, I tell the truth. I think that helps more than lies when we want to solve problems."

Ladislaw returned home with pain in his heart for the misunderstanding, and malice that he experienced in this meeting. It seemed nobody wants to support him with his struggle, only criticizing him for his activity. Some of the people because of their enviousness, and some of them because of their fear of the central power. They tried to isolate themselves from the actual problems. He thought; I hope I did something good, while I got a few medals for my work. While some gypsy leaders like to talk so much, they didn't do the right things. Talk is cheap, acting is the prove of saying. I sacrificed my life for my village, and now we have the results, rightfully. He went to talk and consolation to his brother, Mike. He was a constructor, and he helped to rebuild their village. When he heard about this last meeting with the civil rights activist from his brother he said:

"I would avoid the public for a while, because some of them are malicious, and they are not seeing reality. Many of them live in a dark age."

"Don't you ever forget; they are also jealous of you."

"Do your things in the village and for the village because you have many serious plans. We will build the logistic center to organize our produce and the factory for canned goods. That is more than enough for us, for now. We will also organize the demonstration in August, against discrimination, and for humanity."

"You are my favorite brother; I promise I will never let you down."

They did hug one another, and Ladislaw left him. On the way home he met also with his other brother Paul. He was helping an elderly couple with their backyard. They got a few apple trees, and cherry trees, also grape production. Paul helped them regularly, and they liked Paul, because one day he found old money in their garden, and he gave it to them instead of hiding or stealing it. He asked Ladislaw if he wants to enjoy him for cherry-picking, but he said:

"I got my cherry, and that is Mimi. I am happy with her. After that, he told about his last meeting with the civil rights representatives.

Paul said:

"Easy to talk, but not so easy to act. What kind of results they got in the last twenty years, "That we can't be called gypsies, but minority ethnic group, and here gypsy's criminology does not exist, but criminology is the right expression. That is ridiculous because we are reminded every day at least a hundred times, that we are the gypsies, and we lived like this for more than 600 years, that is all that we got? Don't mind them."

Ladislaw did hug him, and walked home happier, than before.

The following day he got several conversations about their products and their plans, with many different people, from their neighborhood. He was in good mood and felt optimistic. On Thursday, he got a meeting with other gypsy mayors, to organize the demonstration in August, throughout the whole country. They wanted to make a quiet marsh from one end to the other end of the country and carry the sign:

"We are also humans; we are one nation."

The leaders told him that they are afraid that the central power will hinder the demonstration.

Ladislaw said:

"I know that can be dangerous, but still worth to try, otherwise we can't take a step forward for the gypsies."

He cited: "The brave man is not the one, who never fear, but the one who can overcome his fear."

Our race lives in misery, and contempt by most of the country. We see it, and we have to do something about it."

After this meeting, he got a call from one of the reporters, and she said:

"I saw your meeting on the Internet with the civil rights activist, and I was surprised by their enviousness."

The things they told, they had put in a different content your doings, they were unjust with you, and with your work. They did not show any respect for you or your good job, and I am sorry for that. Otherwise, if they got to say important things, they should talk to you privately in your office, and not try to destroy your reputation publicly, to appreciate the many good things you did.

Ladislaw said:

"Thank you for your empathy, we are thinking the same."

I got it now, I know them, and I will consider their opinions in the future. Everybody is entitled to have an opinion, but that also shows who is the person. Their result after more than 600 years of gypsy's misery, that the people may not call us gypsy, instead Romani, or "minority ethnic group", and gypsy's crime does not exist, only the criminology, as a whole subject. Too bad, we are reminded that we are gypsies at least a hundred times a day. What I experienced in several prisons, it does not count, because I did not use the right terminology: "Minority ethnic groups." They did not know, but I was visiting prisons in many places, not only the three of our county because I wanted to know more about the gypsies living conditions. For sure the old saying is true:

"Who needs enemies, if I have friends like they are."

"I just hope, they will wake up before it will be too late. "Acts are speaking louder than words. A "miracle" is not happening from itself, people have to work for it, and be prepared for it."

"Thank you for your call, goodbye."

Mimi arrived at the end of the day, and they walked out with Ladislaw because they visited Mimi's sister for dinner. Her sister was a nurse in the hospital, and they conversed about the shortages of several medical supplies, and what they got, they must use it longer than they should. Mimi's sister Dena liked Ladislaw to being honest. They also talked about the president's style that he had close several media's post, and news-paper productions also.

Dena said:

"It seems that the freedom of the press is gone for now."

She continued:

"Our president doesn't like to hear the truth because he does not want to have justice, make changes, or repair his mistakes. He also said, they can exist in the parliament without the opponent parties. We got earlier a president like him, but he got a sad finish for his dictatorship. The president lives in the middle age, like no positive changes for the poor, down with the gypsies, and no news, no power for any others. In case someone tries to be too smart, can hang himself, or they will help him, as I heard."

Ladislaw said:

"The most difficult thing is the self-criticism, and the recreation of ourselves."

"I could experience it in my life, but at least I tried to do it, and I repaired my mistakes."

"Self-actualization has to live with us in our days, we have to adapt to new situations, the autocracy leads to negative consequences."

Dena said:

"I am very proud of you, because you did many good things, and because you stayed true to yourself," Ladislaw said:

"Thank you much for your kindness, and now we have to go, goodbye"

They went for a walk after dinner with Mimi and they saw a girl had slept by a man. They did not like it, and they went closer to ask what is going on. The girl was gypsy, and she cried. She told, that the man invited her for a drink, and wanted sex with her right away, but she said "No."

"The man hit her, and now he left."

Ladislaw went after the man, and told him:

"What kind of human-being are you to hit a young girl?"

The man said:

"She was flirting, and later she said: "No."

Ladislaw said:

"I don't call the police this time, but she is my relative, I don't want to see you next to her anymore. I hope you got it."

The man said:

"Get the hell out of my way" and walked off.

Ladislaw introduced himself to the girl, and Mimi told her to come over on the weekend for a chatter. Mimi was very proud of Ladislaw, and she said:

"You are my hero."

Ladislaw said:

"Thank you much, but I would like to be also all the gypsies hero because that is the purpose of my life. What is life good for if we can't live freely."

Mimi said:

"I can see that, and I pray to God to save you on your way."

Ladislaw said:

"Don't forget, on Sunday we are invited to my friend's Joe's wedding."

Mimi said:

"I do not want to miss anything, where I can learn." They said "Goodbye", because they arrived at Mimi's home. Ladislaw did not go in, because Mimi's mom was already sleeping, although he was tempted. He returned his home sad and tired.

On Sunday, the weather was sunny, and the sky was blue. It was perfect for the occasion. They went to the wedding; the place was beautiful with many flowers with green and white ornaments. The young couple was smiley, and happy when Ladislaw arrived with Mimi. Both were looking very nice, and Ladislaw wore his new shirt from the secondhand shop. Mimi had a nice blue dress, with a pink rose in her hair.

Ladislaw said:

"I hope our wedding will be nice too in September. What do you think?"

Mimi said:

"I can hardly wait for the moment to say "yes" to you. Someday I feel like, it will never happen."

They eat a lot and laugh a lot, they also got a gypsy band, and they played beautifully. Some of the people had a dance. Suddenly the band started to play the Toselli Serenade. That was Mimi's favorite song.

Mimi asked Ladislaw:

"Did you order it for me?"

Ladislaw said:

"Yes, I like to see you be always happy."

Mimi asked him:

"How comes that you didn't advise anybody to be a musician in your village?"

Ladislaw answered:

"I wanted to make sure that my people in the village never have to starve, therefore, I think they are more secured with the products they make. Any fool can spend money, but not everybody can make it." "I love music but hard to make these days money with the music, when four million people are in deep poverty in our land."

"By the way, my smaller brother is playing on the guitar" Mimi has giggled, and she said:

"That didn't sound too romantic, my darling."

Ladislaw said:

"Believe me, I am very romantic with you, while I must keep my head for my village's sake."

They left the party earlier because Mimi wanted Ladislaw to make love to her. She was hungry for his love and sometimes she felt jealous of the village.

She said:

"We might live for us only today, who knows what happens tomorrow."

Ladislaw said:

"I am happy that you are so loving, and natural, who could say no to you?"

The following day Mimi went to visit her grandmother in the other village, and she arrived on the next day afternoon when she got the tragic news.

CHAPTER 3

Monday, early afternoon was a secret call for Ladislaw, and after that, he left his office. The following day he disappeared, and the people look for him, but they did not find him anywhere. They went to the police, and after that, they found him in the old mayor's office, which they used as a storage. Ladislaw was hanging from the ceiling. They told, he killed himself. That was unrealistic, with so many good results, and an important future, and what he told in his interview in May. He said:

"I will never give up my fight for the gypsies, and the poor."

After he died, in the news they told that he was ill, but he never talked about it. They said maybe he was hopelessly in love with somebody. These all were also against the facts, only guessings. Anyway, what is true? He was hopelessly in love, or sick? He was not a teenage boy with his forty-six years of age, just for nothing to commit suicide. Why did he never talk about sickness or doctor visits? He had many plans for the following weeks, and he was looking healthy, and ambitious. Notwithstanding his busy work schedule, he always behaved nicely and understanding with everybody. He was always patient, and benevolent. He was a talented, fulfilled, and a young person with a bright future. The other very suspicious thing is that lately, too many important people committed suicide in Wonderland.

That was already, like an epidemy. Death by hanging does not leave a trace, especially if someone holds a gun to their head. It is hard to prove afterward if anybody else did it. Some people said that the last phone call was critical, maybe they invited Ladislaw to negotiate, and instead, that was his hanging. All his relatives and friends were shocked, and his mom was crying nonstop, and she kept saying:

"Why did you do it my son, why? "Everybody loved you, and you did a good job for the village, and all the gypsies."

After our accomplishment, nobody can say that the gypsies are useless, or no good."

Mimi was out of herself, she passed out when she heard the news. The funeral was a drama for everybody, and thousands of people arrived to show their love, and sympathy, in this village with only four hundred people.

Some said:

"He knew too much, probably they killed him."

Nobody knew anything for sure, the only thing everybody said, it was " unbelievable." Ladislaw died, but he will always live in the heart and mind of the people, who will fight for their justice, and against poverty, discrimination, and prejudice. In the twist of our life, we realize only later that our faith is written in our blood. The countries are not black or white, they are beautiful, because of the different races can exist peacefully together in diversity.

"Ladislaw was a great human-being of our time, God bless him", -said the priest, and he continued:

"May his struggle never go in vain, and he will live always in the heart of his people. He gave hope, inspiration, and strength to everybody around him. He, who did not accept defeat in his whole life, would give up, that seems impossible and bewildering for all of us. God bless you, my son."

After the funeral they talked about Ladislaw in all forums, most of them are posted on the Internet. Also, the previous ambassador of India, who met with Ladislaw, and knew him, he wrote a beautiful article on the Internet, and he cited what Ladislaw told him:

"I will fade away one day, but the Romani folks will receive all the attention they deserve," Maybe, he was a poster boy of the Romani community in the mainstream media, but he died as a hero of the whole nation. He will be always the best "ambassador" of his people in their future fights. He stood firm, and he had a fight with all his heart, and mind for the Romanis, and he also did fight against unjust, and prejudice. God bless his soul. Many people did not want to believe that Ladislaw committed suicide, therefore the police investigated longer. They walked on the streets of the village and asked questions. What may they find, the traces are all disappeared. They should right away order criminologists to help. It would be better to know the truth. Many people were very sad, and upset because Ladislaw did not show any signs of illness or depression. Just the opposite, he got many plans for the coming months already.

The village was mourning, and they felt left alone with their fight. They also were afraid of what the future hold for them. Some people said, the ruling class paid professional killers to hang him, but we never will know it. Ladislaw went to heaven for his kindness, goodwill, and help because God loved him. At the same time, the president of Wonderland did not find any words to say about him, like who cares about him. He created a loveless, and money-oriented society, but that will be his "Karma," later. The better people still care for someone, who was nice, benevolent, and famous. He got many appreciation medals, given by people for his work.

Ladislaw could not see the consequences of the ugly treatment that he got by some of the people of his race. Some gypsies hated him, and they did not show any interest in his success, and kindness They showed only malice and enviousness. Nobody knew where his story will end, while he fought against unfavorable odds most of his time, but suicide was not on the people's mind. His family wanted to keep Ladislaw's death private. They said:" People should remember about his life, and not about his death." They had probably more reasons for that.

Ladislaw earned to be the hero of the gypsies all over the world, not only in Wonderland. His death was bewildering for everybody who loved him, especially for his family and his village. They felt like they lost with him also their future.

Heroes do not ask, they fight, and they do not know fear, because they believe in the goodness and the victory of their nation. God will be with them always.